Bordaria
Difendere con Coraggio

**Scholastic Canada Ltd.**
604 King Street West, Toronto, Ontario M5V 1E1, Canada

**Scholastic Inc.**
557 Broadway, New York, NY 10012, USA

**Scholastic Australia Pty Limited**
PO Box 579, Gosford, NSW 2250, Australia

**Scholastic New Zealand Limited**
Private Bag 94407, Botany, Manukau 2163, New Zealand

**Scholastic Children's Books**
Euston House, 24 Eversholt Street, London NW1 1DB, UK

# PÖP & F!ZZ

Published by Pop & Fizz and Scholastic Australia in 2010.
Pop & Fizz is a partnership between Paddlepop Press and Lemonfizz Media.
www.paddlepoppress.com
Text, design and illustrations copyright © Lemonfizz Media 2010.
Cover illustration by Melanie Matthews.
Internal illustrations by Lionel Portier, Melanie Matthews, Steve Karp and James Hart

First published by Scholastic Australia in 2010.
This edition published by Scholastic Canada Ltd. in 2012.

**Library and Archives Canada Cataloguing in Publication**
Park, Mac
Sludgia / by Mac Park.
(Boy vs beast. Battle of the worlds)
ISBN 978-1-4431-1903-0
I. Title. II. Series: Park, Mac. Boy vs beast. Battle of the worlds.
PZ7.P2213Sl 2012      j823'.92      C2012-901471-0

6 5 4 3 2 1      Printed in Canada 116      12 13 14 15 16

# BOY vs BEAST

## BATTLE OF THE BORDERS

# SLUDGIA

## Mac Park

POP & FIZZ

SCHOLASTIC

# Prologue

Long ago beast and man shared one world. Then battles began between them.

After many battles, the world was split in two. Beasts were given Beastium. Man was given Earth.

A border-wall was made. It closed the two worlds off.

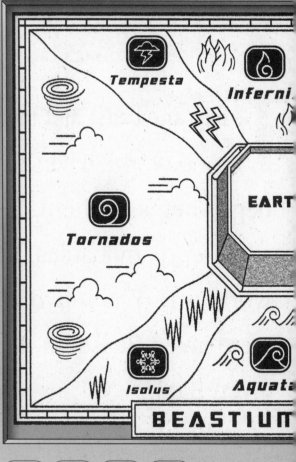

Tempesta

Inferni.

EARTH

Tornados

Isolus

Aquata

BEASTIUM

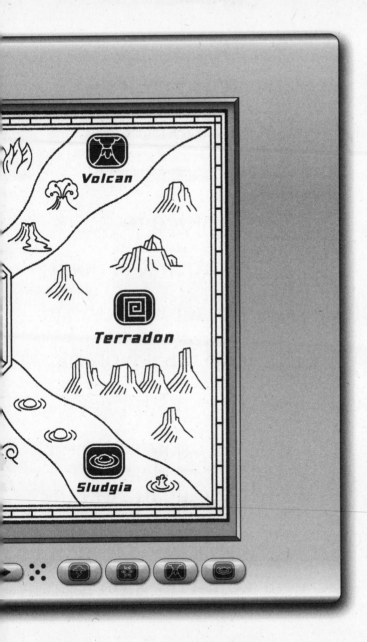

Volcan

Terradon

Sludgia

**B**order Guards were trained to defend the border-wall.

The beasts tried to get through the border-wall many times. The Border Guards had to stop them. Battles won by beasts made them stronger. Battles won by guards earned them new battle gear. And they got new upgrades. Then their battle gear could do more.

Five boys now defend the border-wall. They are in training to become Border Masters. Just like their dads.

Their dads were also Border Guards once. Then they became Border Captains and then Border Knights. They kept learning until they became Border Masters. Now they make up the Bordaria Master Command. The BMC.

The BMC helped the Border Guards during battle. They gave the Border Guards new battle gear.

The boys had to earn new battle gear. They needed to learn from their battles. And from their mistakes.

Kai Masters is a Border Guard. His work is top secret. The BMC watch Kai closely. Kai must not fail.

# The Beastium Border-Lands

The beasts of Beastium lived in four lands. There was a fire land. There was a rock land and a water land. And there was an air land.

But over time, the edges of the lands mixed. That was how the border-lands were made.

The edges of fire and rock mixed. That made a volcano land. The edges of rock and water mixed. That made a mud border-land.

The edges of water and wind mixed. That made an ice border-land. The edges of wind and fire mixed. That made a storm border-land.

But it was not just the edges of the worlds that mixed.

The beasts from each of the worlds mixed, too. And then a new kind of beast was made . . .

The border-land beast.

Kai Masters must think about his old battles. He must learn from them. If he does not, then he will fail.

Kai must not lose.

# Chapter 1

It was Sunday morning.
Kai Masters was at the dog
park. He was playing with his
dog. But Kai's dog was not just
any dog. It was a dogbot.
And Kai was not just any
12-year-old kid. He was a
Border Guard.

It was Kai's job to guard the border-wall. He had to stop beasts from breaking through it. Kai had to keep the beasts in their own lands. His dogbot, BC3, helped him.

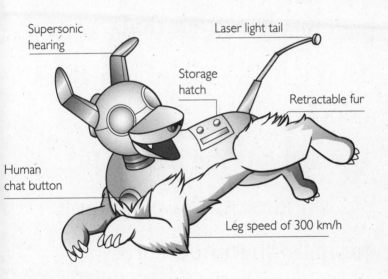

Supersonic hearing

Laser light tail

Storage hatch

Retractable fur

Human chat button

Leg speed of 300 km/h

BC could move fast. And he could talk. But only when Kai turned on his chat button.

BC loved going to the dog park. When he went there he wore his fake fur. It made him look just like other dogs. No one could tell he was a dogbot.

Kai threw the ball for BC. BC ran after it. BC picked up the ball. Then he heard,

**Splat!**

Mud splats were hitting the ground.

**Splat!
Splotch!**

*Strange*, thought BC.

He ran back to Kai.

"Where's the ball?" asked Kai. BC barked. Then he ran off again.

*He wants me to go with him*, thought Kai. He was about to go after BC when he heard,

**Splat!**

Mud had fallen onto a boy's head. *Where did that come from?* thought Kai.

**Splat! Splat! Squelch!**

Suddenly there was mud

falling down on everyone.

Nearly everyone had mud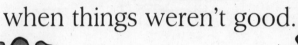
in their hair. They ran for cover.
Kai looked up. The mud was
falling from the sky. *But how?*
thought Kai.

BC came back with the ball.
He had mud in his fake fur.

"Yuck!" said Kai. Then he
saw BC's tail. It was wagging.
BC always wagged his tail
when things weren't good.

"You're right, BC," said Kai. "This has to be coming from a beast."

Kai took out his orbix. The BMC gave one to all their Border Guards.

It was a small computer. The BMC used them to talk with their guards.

Sometimes Kai used his orb to store things. Things that he wanted to learn about. And Kai wanted to learn about this mud.

Kai keyed in,

**Get sample**

A metal hand shot out from the orb.

It grabbed the mud on BC's fur. Then it went back inside the orb.

Kai turned BC's chat button on. "We need to test this mud," said Kai.

"Yes," said BC. "In the lab at home."

# Chapter 2

Kai lived in a lighthouse.
There were rooms above the
ground. And there were rooms
under the ground.

The rooms under the ground
were secret Border Guard
rooms. It was there that Kai
learned about beasts. And about
Beastium.

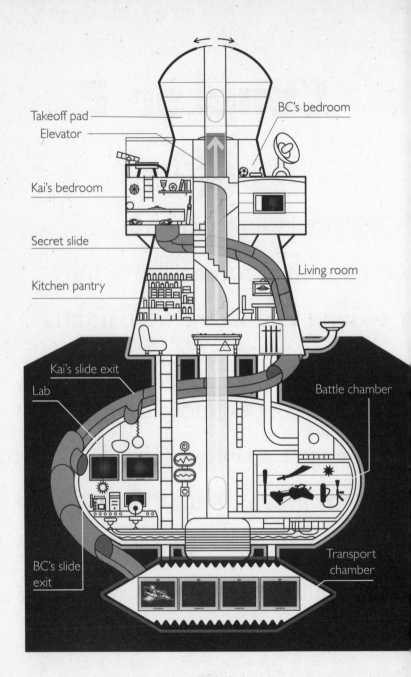

Takeoff pad

Elevator

BC's bedroom

Kai's bedroom

Secret slide

Kitchen pantry

Living room

Kai's slide exit

Lab

Battle chamber

BC's slide exit

Transport chamber

Kai and BC went into the kitchen pantry. Kai felt under the bottom shelf. He found a button and pressed it.

The back wall of the pantry began to move. Behind the wall was a ladder. Kai and BC went down the ladder into the lab.

The lab was filled with computers and tools.

Kai put the mud into the sample tester.

The computer screen
flashed.

"The water land and the
rock land," said Kai. Then the
screen flashed once more.
"Sludgia," said Kai.

"The border-land between the rock and water lands. That's a very muddy land."

Kai hit the Sludgia button.

A card popped up on the screen.

"This beast looks angry," said Kai. "Come on, BC. It's time for us to go get dirty."

**BEAST I.D.**

## MUDAMINISAUR
This little beast can play dirty

Strength ★★★★★

Attack Power ★★★★★

Speed ★★★★★

# Chapter 3

Behind the lab was another secret room. It was the battle chamber. All the battle gear was kept there.

"Can I open the battle chamber?" asked BC.

"Yes," said Kai.

The BMC had given BC a Border Guard Buddy Card.

The card was a prize.
BC had done good work in
battle. BC's card was just like
Kai's Border Guard Card. It let
them into the battle chamber.

Name........... **Biotic Canine 3**
Owner.......... **BG Kai Masters**
Guard Post... **Lighthouse**
Rank............ **Border Guard Buddy**

34361452

BC pushed his card into the computer slot with his paw. Some bricks in the lab wall began to move.

**CLUNK! BANG!**

**Whiiiiir! BANG!**

They made a space like a small door. Kai and BC stepped though the space.

There were three walls in the battle chamber.

Kai had used a lot of things on wall one. He looked at wall three. Kai went to take something. He heard a noise.

## CLUNK GRRR CLUNK

Then a computer voice said,

## Not yet!

"When?" asked BC.

"I don't know," said Kai.

"But look at that thing on wall two. That's what we need."

## MAXI-2 HEAT BLASTER

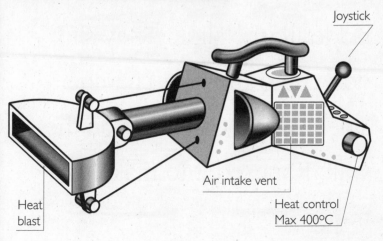

Joystick

Air intake vent

Heat blast

Heat control Max 400ºC

"This will dry out mud," said Kai. "I wonder if we can have something else?"

The computer voice said,

## No more from here

## Take slide to transport chamber.

Kai and BC climbed the ladder to the slide. They slid down into the next chamber. There was a computer on the wall. Kai used it to make his transport.

"Time to build our ride, BC," said Kai. He pressed the start button on the BG Build-a-Ride.

"We will be on the ground in a mud land," said Kai. He hit the land button.

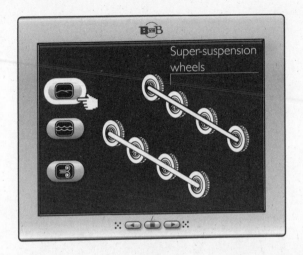

Then he hit the mud button.

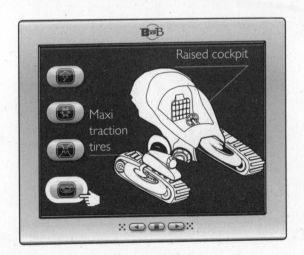

# Then he hit the digger.

Sludge mode NOW READY

Digger tray

Bot mode
NOT YET

Mud ball
paddles

Turbo inflatable
tires

"It will be good for mud battle," said BC.

"I hope so," said Kai.

Part of the floor behind them began to move. It was in the middle of the room.

## Brrrrrr Brrrrrr

The bit of floor slid open. It left a big hole. Up from the hole came the sludger. The one that Kai had just made.

"It's just right," said Kai.

He and BC jumped inside.

Kai took out his orb. He put it into the orb-shaped space in the dashboard.

"We will need to win battle

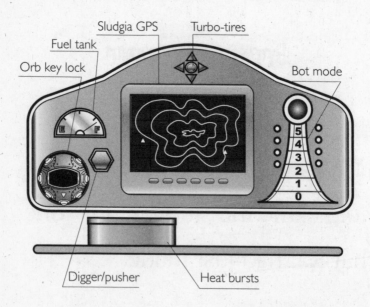

Fuel tank

Sludgia GPS

Turbo-tires

Orb key lock

Bot mode

Digger/pusher

Heat bursts

points," said BC.

"Yes," said Kai. "Then we can change it to a bot. This bot mode screen will tell us when."

Kai pushed the button. The elevator began to move. It took Kai and BC to the top of the lighthouse. The elevator doors opened.

The sludger was on the takeoff pad.

Kai keyed in the codes for Sludgia on his orb. Then he hit the light button.

The roof of the lighthouse opened. The takeoff pad filled with light. The light shot up into the sky.

It took Kai, BC and the sludger with it. To the border-land of Sludgia.

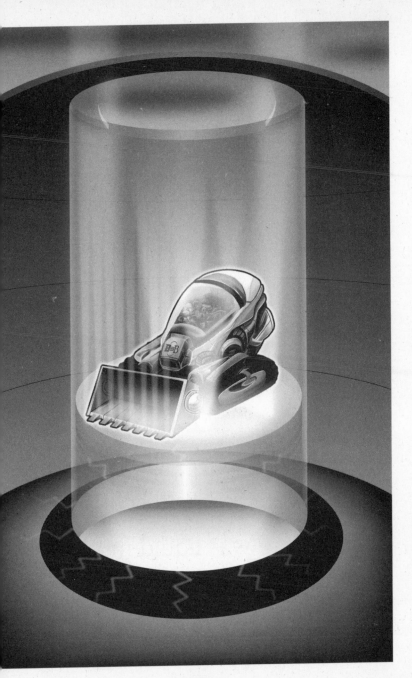

# Chapter 4

The sludger landed in a pool of mud.

**Squelch!**
**Squelch!**

Kai looked around.
They were on the top of a hill. There was liquid mud everywhere. It was running

down over rocks.

Mud flowed like a river along the ground. It spilled over cliffs like falls of water.

"Lucky we have these big wheels," said Kai. "They won't get stuck in the mud." But Kai was wrong. The sludger had landed hard in the mud. It had sunk deep into it. And it was stuck.

"We're not moving," said BC.

"I know," said Kai. "The mud is too thick." Kai hit the turbo-tires button on the dashboard. The wheels suddenly grew bigger.

The sludger rose up out of the mud. Then Kai drove it down the hill.

"We won points for that!" said BC. "Look at the bars."

Kai looked at the dashboard and smiled.

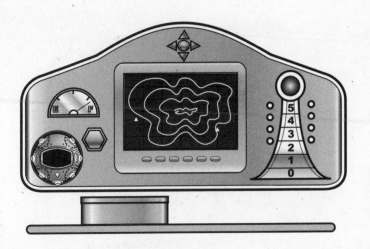

At the bottom of the hill was a sea of mud. "It's not deep," said Kai. "We can push it out of the way."

Kai set the sludger to pusher. The digger tray flipped over.

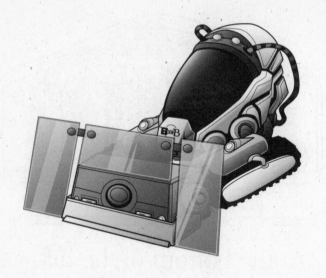

They drove into the sea of mud. The pusher pushed the mud out of the way.

"Good," said Kai. "We'll be able to change to bot mode soon. But where is the beast?"

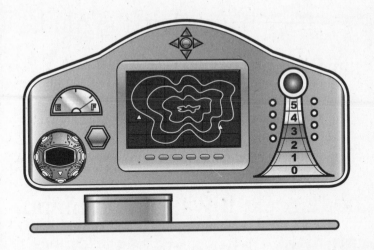

All at once, mud flew up
into the air. Kai stopped and
looked. The mud shot up from
the ground.

Kai moved around the mud.
The pusher hit something hard.

"It's a big rock in the mud," said Kai.

But BC's tail was wagging. The rock began to move. It was not a rock. It was a mud hippo. The mud hippo spun its tail fast.

Mud balls flew from its tail.
Mud, mud and more mud.
It went everywhere. Kai couldn't
see where he was going.
Before he knew it, he had hit
another one. The rock moved.
It was a mud hippo, too. A tail
shot up and began to spin.

Splat!
Splat!
Splat!

"We need to get out of here, BC," said Kai. "Without waking up more mud hippos!"

"But we can't see," said BC. "Mud is all over sludger."

"We have a body-heat finder," said Kai. "It's in the computer." Kai turned the finder on. The dashboard screen looked like a computer game.

All the mud hippos were on the screen.

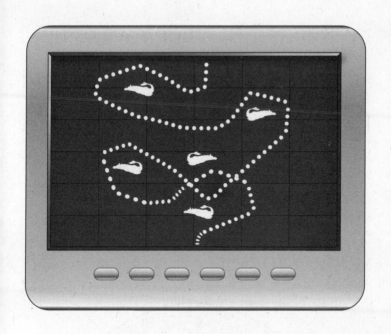

A dotted line showed Kai
how to go between the
mud hippos.

Kai began driving. He drove
slowly through the hippos.

Kai and BC didn't wake up any more of them. "Phew," said Kai. "That was tricky."

"But now bars are full," said BC. "We can change from sludger to bot."

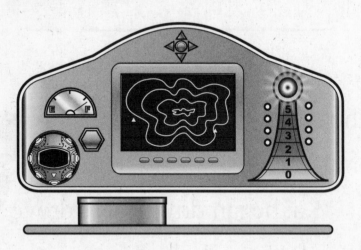

All of a sudden the river of mud moved faster. Faster and faster it went. And as it moved, it took rocks with it. *They look like rock-land rocks,* thought Kai.

Mud and rock moved together. Mud flew and rocks rolled. It was hard to see. And then there was a huge noise.

# Chapter 5

A beast stood in front of Kai and BC. It was a huge pile of mud and rock. And the beast pulled more mud and rock into it. As it did, it grew bigger and bigger. It growled.

## GGGGRRRR

Kai knew that growl.

*It sounds like the rock beast from the rock land,* he thought. He took a photo with the orb.

**BvsB** **BEAST I.D.**

**MUDAMEGASAUR**
Beware the mud sling attack

| Strength | ★★★★★ |
| --- | --- |
| Attack Power | ★★★★★ |
| Speed | ★★★★★ |

"This is a big beast," said Kai. "It's not the beast in the lab. It's changed." Then the beast turned on Kai.

**WOOSh WOOSh**

Huge mud balls flew into the air. They hit the sludger hard.

**BANG! BANG! BANG!**

The sludger rolled.
Kai put the sludger back up on

its wheels again.

"Are you all right, BC?"

"All right," said BC.
"But beast is doing more
mud-sling attacks!"

"Yes," said Kai. "We have to
stop it."

## HEAT BURSTS

On impact gives
off 5000 degree
Celsius heat bursts

"I'll use the
Maxi-heat blaster,"
said Kai.
"You use the
heat bursts."

Kai opened the cockpit. BC grabbed the box of heat bursts. He threw a heat burst at the beast. It hit it in the neck. There was a big noise.

# KABOOM!

The heat burst popped open. Heat burst out of the beast like there was a fire.

The heat dried out the mud

on the beast's neck.
There was just rock
left.

BC threw
more heat bursts. Kai used
the heat blaster.
Together, they dried
up all the beast's mud.

There was nothing left
of it but a pile of
rocks. "Go, us!"
said Kai.

Kai drove the sludger up to the pile of rocks. Then he used the digger to pick up the rocks.

"Let's throw these rocks into the rock land," said Kai. And he started driving away from the mud.

Suddenly BC's tail wagged. "Watch out!" said BC. But it was too late. Kai had hit another mud hippo.

This time the mud hippo's

tail didn't spin. It came out of the mud. It scooped up the pile of rocks in the digger. And it took them down into the mud with it.

"This won't be good," said Kai.

# Chapter 6

The mud bubbled. There was a strange sucking sound.

## SLURP

A beast rose from the mud.

"It's changed again," said Kai.

"Maybe time for us to change, too?" said BC. "Change to bot."

"Yes," said Kai. He hit the button to change. Then he took a photo with his orb. A card popped up on the screen.

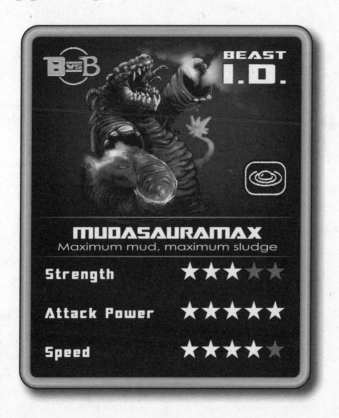

ai blasted heat into the beast's hands. It
ried up the mud. And it stopped the mud hurls.

Use your eye
asers on its other
hand, BC.

It's working.
No more mud balls!

GROOOARRRR!

ut the beast was very angry. It sucked
pools of mud. It was getting ready
r a mud-wave attack.

A mud-wave attack!
Quick, let's go.

We're not going
to make it!

Kai and BC were high up on the cliff. On one side was Sludgia. On the other was Aquatan.

This is where Sludgia was made.

But where do we go now? We are stuck.

The beast sent a giant wave attack into the cliff. It covered everything in its path with hurling mud.

CRASH!

We have to jump. It will push us into Aquatan if we don't.

# Chapter 7

The bot was sinking fast.
Mud had almost covered the
cockpit. Kai pushed the turbo-
tires. The bot rose up.
But then it stopped. It was still
up to its chest in mud.

"We have to use heat," said
Kai. "Quick! We have to dry up
the mud."

BC threw heat bursts.
Kai used the Maxi-heat blaster.

"It's working," said BC.
"The mud is turning to dirt."

"Now we can climb out," said Kai.

"We need to climb that cliff again, BC," said Kai. "I know what to do with this beast. Start barking, BC."

BC barked. The beast turned and looked.

The bot began to climb the rocks.

Kai heard a growl.

# GGGGRRRR!

The beast was very mad. It chased them up the cliff.

The bot made it to the top. Kai changed the bot back to sludger mode. He drove the sludger into a small cave. And waited.

The beast stood on the top of the cliff. It looked for Kai and BC.

"We have to be quick, BC," said Kai. "You work the pusher-tray. I'll drive."

Kai put the sludger into turbo-charge.

Kai put his foot down hard on the pedal. The sludger flew out from the cave. It hit the beast from behind.

The pusher pushed the beast over the cliff. Over the cliff and into Aquatan.

SPLASH!

Kai put the brakes on. He and BC climbed out. They looked over the edge of the cliff.

The beast floated away in the Aquatan water. And it was breaking apart. Soon it would be nothing but water.

They hoped.

# Chapter 8

"The border-wall is safe again, BC," said Kai.

"Mud beast is all washed up," said BC.

"Yes," said Kai. "Let's get back into the sludger. It's home time now."

Kai pushed the button on the orb for home.

White light shot down from the sky. It fell on the sludger. The light shot back up into the sky. It took the sludger with it. In the blink of an eye they were gone. Back home to the lighthouse.

# MUDASAURAMAX

This beast is all washed up

| Battle Plays | ★★★☆☆ |
|---|---|
| New Attacks | ★☆☆☆☆ |
| Energy | ★☆☆☆☆ |

# Kai Masters

Kai slogs the sludge!

| | |
|---|---|
| **Battle Plays** | ★★★☆☆ |
| **Upgrades** | ★★☆☆☆ |

**Border Guard Level**

**Games, sneak peeks and more!**

**Can you beat the Boy Vs Beast high score?**

# BATTLE OF THE WORLDS

**BOY vs BEAST**

**BATTLE OF THE BORDERS**

**TEMPESTA**

**Will Kai and his Jet-Charge be able to stop the storm beast?**

**Don't miss the first book in the Battle of the Borders.**